Wee Three Pigs

Grosset & Dunlap

*Hogs and Kisses
and a very Pig thank you
to my good friends
Kathy Wiechman,
Sue Koenig,
and Linda Doughman—H.P.*

Text and illustrations copyright © 2002 by Heidi Petach. All rights reserved.
Published by Grosset & Dunlap, a division of Penguin Putnam Books for Young Readers, New York.
GROSSET & DUNLAP is a trademark of Penguin Putnam Inc. Published simultaneously in Canada.
Printed in the U.S.A.

Library of Congress Cataloging-in-Publication Data is available.

ISBN 0-448-42528-9   A B C D E F G H I J

Wee Three Pigs

By Heidi Petach

Grosset & Dunlap, Publishers

One day their mother told them, "It's time to find jobs and build your own homes. But watch out for the wolf! He'd love to have roast pig for his Christmas dinner."

So the three little pigs packed their bags and
kissed their mother goodbye. Then they set out to
make their way in the pig wide world.

Comet, the first little pig, loved computers. He was too busy to worry about the wolf. So he just made a flimsy house from cardboard boxes.

Unfortunately, Comet's first customer was the wolf. "Little pig, little pig, let me in!" called the wolf. "I need to upgrade my PC."

But Comet wasn't fooled. "Not by the hair on my chinny chin chin!" he squealed.

"Then I'll huff and I'll puff and I'll BLOW your house down!" shouted the wolf. And he did! He huffed and he puffed and he blew those boxes flat as a laptop.

Comet streaked out of there so fast, he slid down the hill to his sister Cupid's house. Cupid lived in a candy shop she had built from peppermint sticks. It looked delicious, but it wasn't very sturdy.

The wolf soon arrived on his sled. "Little pig, little pig, let me in!" he called to Cupid. "I need to buy Christmas candy for my sweetheart."

But Cupid wasn't fooled. "Not by the hair on my chinny chin chin!" she shot back.

"Then I'll huff and I'll puff and I'll BLOW your house down!" shouted the wolf. And he did! He huffed and he puffed until the air exploded with candy.

Zing! Comet and Cupid zipped out of there so fast,
they slid all the way to their brother Rudolph's house.

Rudolph sold electric lights and lived in a sturdy brick house. He had built it especially to withstand wolf-force winds.

The three little pigs were enjoying mugs of hot, spiced
slop when the wolf arrived. "Little pig, little pig, let me in!"
sang the wolf. "I'm awfully cold from Christmas caroling."

But Rudolph wasn't fooled. "Hogwash!" he snorted.
"Not by the hair on my chinny chin chin!"

"Then I'll huff and I'll puff and I'll BLOW your house down!"
shouted the wolf.

So the wolf huffed and he puffed. He nearly turned inside-out, but it was no use. The house was still standing. He finally left in a big huff.

LOOKS LIKE HE BLEW IT!

"Yay!" cried the pigs, rooting for themselves. "Let's celebrate!"

So the three little pigs had a great time "bacon" Christmas cookies,

decorating the tree,

and singing "We Three Pigs of Oreos Are."

Suddenly, there was an awful racket coming from the roof. "I bet that it's Santa Claus!" Cupid exclaimed.

"Yes, it's Santa CLAWS!" cried the wolf. And there he was, dressed in a Santa suit, headed for the chimney!

But Rudolph was not fooled. He sneaked outside and saw who was really on the roof. "Quick! Stretch open the stocking!" Rudolph cried to his sister and brother as the wolf scrambled down the chimney.

Plop! The wolf was bagged and tied. But what should they do with him? "Call the police!" cried Comet.

"Wait! Did he bring us any presents?" asked Cupid hopefully. The wolf shook his head. He looked a little ashamed as a tear slid down Cupid's cheek.

Rudolph asked, "Why do you want to eat us for Christmas dinner? We never did anything to you."

The wolf had a lump in his throat, but it wasn't from roast pig. "It's wolf tradition to pig out on Christmas," he said. "But now that I've met you, I would feel bad about eating you."

AWW—
I'M GETTING
ALL WARM
AND FUZZY!

For a long time, no one spoke. Slowly, together, they watched a tiny star twinkle bigger and brighter till it seemed to light up the whole sky.

"We have a tradition, too," said Rudolph as dawn began to glow. "We share Christmas breakfast with our friends."

And so they did. And the wolf was careful not to eat the three little pigs or to wolf down his pancakes too fast. He was even polite when Comet hogged the syrup.

This isn't The End. It's just the beginning of a new friendship.